Tales of FATE

Retold Timeless Classics

COVER-TO-COVER BOOKS

Perfection Learning®

Retold by Paula J. Reece
Illustrator: Bill Ersland
Cover and Book Design: Deborah Lea Bell

For information, contact
Perfection Learning® Corporation
1000 North Second Avenue, P.O. Box 500
Logan, Iowa 51546-0500.
Phone: 800-831-4190 • Fax: 712-644-2392

Paperback ISBN 0-7891-5308-4
Cover Craft® ISBN 0-7807-9678-0
Printed in the U.S.A.
4 5 6 7 8 PP 08 07 06 05

Contents

The Interlopers

Based on the story by Saki

Fate brings two enemies together one stormy night. It's a night they have both prayed for. However, the enemies have a change of heart. They decide to twist fate. But is it ever really possible to stop fate once the ball starts rolling?

A man stood one winter night in a forest in Europe. He was watching and listening. He seemed to wait for some animal to come within the range of his rifle. But the game he waited for wasn't featured in any hunter's magazine. Ulrich von Gradwitz patrolled the dark forest in search of a human enemy.

Ulrich owned a large amount of forestland. And it was well stocked with game. But there was one strip of land that he guarded most jealously. Not because it was special in any way. But because of a feud.

In the days of his grandfather, a neighboring family had claimed that they owned the land. But in a famous lawsuit, the judge had found in favor of the von Gradwitz family. However, the neighbors had never accepted the judge's ruling. So a long series of poaching conflicts had made the families enemies for three generations.

The neighbor feud had become more personal with Ulrich as head of his family. If there was a man in the world whom he hated and wished harm to, it was Georg Znaeym. Georg had inherited the quarrel in his family.

The feud might have, perhaps, died down if it weren't for the personal grudges of the two men. As boys, they had thirsted for each other's blood. As men, each prayed that misfortune might befall the other.

And on this night, Ulrich knew that Georg and his thieves were prowling in his forest. A storm was brewing. Normally, the deer would keep hidden during weather like this. But tonight they were running like they were mad. Something was disturbing the creatures of the forest. And Ulrich could guess what.

Ulrich had posted watchers at the top of a hill. Then he strayed away by himself. He peered through tree trunks and listened through the whistling of the wind. He was searching for any sight or sound of the trespassers.

If only on this wild night, in this dark, lone spot, he might come across Georg Znaeym. Man-to-man. With no one to witness. This wish was first in his thoughts. He stepped around the trunk of a huge beech tree. And he came face-to-face with the man he sought.

The two enemies stood glaring at each other for a long, silent moment. Each held a rifle in his hand. Each had hate in his heart and murder on his mind. The chance to act out the passions of a lifetime had come.

But it was not easy to shoot down a neighbor in cold blood without a word spoken. So each man hesitated. And before either could act, a deed of nature's own violence overtook them both.

There was a fierce shriek of the storm. Then a splitting crash exploded overhead. Before they could jump out of the way, a huge branch fell on them.

Ulrich was stretched on the ground. One arm was numb beneath him. The other was held almost as helplessly in a tight tangle of forked branches. Both his legs were pinned beneath the fallen mass. Luckily, his heavy hunting boots had saved his feet from being crushed to pieces. But it was obvious he could not move until someone helped him.

At his side lay Georg. He was alive and struggling. But he was as helplessly pinned down as Ulrich. All around them lay a wreckage of splintered branches and broken twigs.

Ulrich was relieved to be alive yet frustrated that he was trapped. This brought a strange medley of thank-yous to God and sharp curses.

Georg was nearly blinded by the blood that trickled across his eyes. But he stopped struggling for a moment to listen to his enemy. He gave a short, snarling laugh.

"So, you're not killed, as you should be," said Georg. "But you're stuck, anyway. Stuck tight. How funny. Ulrich von Gradwitz trapped in his stolen forest. There's real justice!"

And Georg laughed again at his enemy.

"I'm caught in my own forestland," replied Ulrich. "My men will come to release us. Then you will wish that you were in a better situation than caught poaching on a neighbor's land."

Georg was silent for a moment. Then he answered quietly, "Are you sure that your men will find much to release? I have men, too, in the forest tonight. They're close behind me. And they will be here first and do the releasing. They will drag me out from under these branches. And then it won't take much to roll this trunk right over on top of you. Your men will find you dead under a fallen beech tree. As a formality, I will send my sympathies to your family."

"My men had orders to follow me in ten minutes," said Ulrich fiercely. "Seven minutes must have already gone by. And when they get me out, I will remember what you said. Only you will have met your death poaching on my land. So I don't think I can decently send any sympathies to your family."

"Good," snarled Georg, "good. We will fight this quarrel out to the death. You and I and our foresters. With no cursed interlopers to come between us. Death to you, Ulrich von Gradwitz."

"The same to you, Georg Znaeym—forest thief, game snatcher."

A Twist of Fate

Each man knew that it might be awhile before his party would seek him out or find him. So it was a matter of chance which men would arrive first on the scene.

Both men had now given up the useless struggle to free themselves. Ulrich used all his effort to free one arm near his outer coat pocket. He took out a wine flask. But even when he had it, it was long before he could manage to unscrew the stopper. Or get any of the liquid down his throat.

But when he did, what a heaven-sent drink it

seemed! It was very cold outside. And the wine warmed and revived the wounded man.

And he then looked across with something like a throb of pity to where his enemy lay. Georg was just barely keeping the groans of pain from crossing his lips.

"Could you reach this flask if I threw it over to you?" Ulrich asked suddenly. "There is good wine in it. We may as well be as comfortable as we can. Let us drink. Even if tonight one of us dies."

"No," said Georg. "I can barely see anything. There is so much blood caked around my eyes. And in any case, I don't drink wine with an enemy."

Ulrich was silent for a few minutes. He lay listening to the screeching of the wind.

An idea was slowly forming and growing in his brain. It gained strength every time he looked across at the man who was fighting so hard against pain and exhaustion. Ulrich's old, fierce hatred seemed to be dying down.

"Neighbor," he said, "do as you please if your men come first. But I've changed my mind. If my men come first, you shall be the first to be helped. As though you were my guest.

"We have quarreled like devils all our lives over this stupid strip of forest," Ulrich continued. "Here where the trees can't even stand up in a breath of wind. Lying here tonight, I've come to think we've been rather foolish. There are better things in life than getting the best of a boundary dispute. Neighbor, if you will help me bury the old quarrel, I—I will ask you to be my friend."

Georg Znaeym was silent. In fact, he was silent so long that Ulrich thought he had fainted. Then Georg spoke slowly.

"Wouldn't the whole region stare and talk if we rode to the market square together?" he said. "No one living can remember seeing a Znaeym and a von Gradwitz talking to each other in friendship. And what peace there would be if we ended our feud tonight. There will be none to interfere, no interlopers from outside . . ."

Georg stopped for a moment. Then he got up enough strength to continue. "You would come and spend New Year's Eve at my house," he said. "And I would come and feast at yours. I would never fire a shot on your land. Except when you invited me as a guest. You could come shoot with me down in the marshes where the wild birds are.

"I never thought I wanted to do any other thing than hate you all my life," Georg continued. "But I think I have changed my mind about things too, this last half hour. And you offered me your wine flask . . . Ulrich von Gradwitz, I will be your friend."

For a time both men were silent. They were thinking about the wonderful changes this dramatic peacemaking would bring about. They lay in the cold, gloomy forest, with the wind tearing in fitful gusts. And they waited for the help that would now bring release to both parties.

And each man made a private prayer. He prayed that his men might be the first to arrive. That way he might be the first to show honorable attention to the enemy who had become a friend.

As the wind died down for a moment, Ulrich broke the silence.

"Let's shout for help," he said. "In this lull, our voices may carry a little way."

"They won't carry far through the trees and brush," said Georg. "But we can try. Together, then."

The two raised their voices in a long hunting call.

"Together again," Ulrich said a few minutes later after hearing no response.

"I heard something that time, I think," said Ulrich.

"I heard nothing but the wind," said Georg hoarsely.

There was silence again for some minutes. Then Ulrich gave a joyful cry.

"I can see figures coming through the woods,"

he said. "They are coming the way I came down the hillside!"

Both men raised their voices in as loud a shout as they could manage.

"They hear us! They've stopped. Now they see us. They're running down the hill toward us!" cried Ulrich.

"How many of them are there?" asked Georg.

"I can't see very well," said Ulrich. "Nine or ten."

"Then they are your men," said Georg. "I had only seven out with me."

"They are running as fast as they can, brave lads," said Ulrich gladly.

"Are they your men?" asked Georg. "Are they your men?" he repeated impatiently.

"No," said Ulrich with a laugh. It was the crazed chattering laugh of a man shaken with hideous fear.

"Who are they?" asked Georg quickly. He was straining his eyes to see what the other gladly would not have seen.

After a short pause, Ulrich answered.

"Wolves."

The Lady, or the Tiger?

Based on the story by Frank R. Stockton

This king thinks he's leaving the fate of his accused citizens in their own hands. Their choices decide their guilt. And what is the fate of the boy who dares to love the king's daughter? That's up to you to decide.

In the very olden time there lived a king. This spirited king had a cruel streak. And he had some crazy ideas. But his people obeyed him so much that his ideas usually became facts.

He usually discussed things with the person he trusted the most—himself. And when he and himself agreed upon anything, the thing was done.

When everything went smoothly, the king was composed and happy. And whenever there was a little hitch, he was even more composed and happier yet. For nothing pleased him more than to make the crooked straight. Or to crush down uneven places.

One of his borrowed ideas was that of a public arena. The arena displayed manly and beastly bravery. This caused his citizens' minds to be refined and cultured.

But even here the king showed his enthusiastic and cruel side. He used the huge stadium for true justice. Crime was punished or innocence rewarded by the laws of something fair and flawless—chance.

If a citizen was accused of a crime, the king decided if it interested him. If it did, then the public was notified. On a certain day the fate of the person would be decided in the king's arena.

On that day all the people gathered in the bleachers. The king would be surrounded by his court. He would sit high on his throne on one side of the arena.

When the king gave a signal, a door beneath

him opened. The accused person stepped out into the arena. Directly across from the accused were two doors. They were exactly alike and side by side. The person on trial had to walk straight to the doors and open one of them.

The person could open either door. But he could receive no help or opinions except from chance itself.

If the accused opened one door, out came a hungry tiger. It would be the fiercest and cruelest that could be captured. It would immediately spring upon him and tear him to pieces. It was a punishment for his guilt.

As soon as the case of the criminal was decided, sad iron bells were clanged in the kingdom. Great cries went up from the hired mourners who were posted on the outer rim of the arena. Then the large audience went slowly home with bowed heads and heavy hearts. They mourned that one so young and fair, or so old and respected, should have deserved such a frightful fate.

But if the accused person opened the other door, out came a lady. She was the most suitable to his age and rank that His Majesty could select among his citizens. And to this lady the accused was instantly married. It was a reward of his innocence.

It didn't matter if he already had a wife and

family. Or if he was already engaged to a woman of his own choosing. The king didn't allow such arrangements to interfere with his great scheme of punishment and reward.

The vows took place right away in the arena. Another door opened beneath the king. A priest was followed by a band of singers and dancing maidens blowing golden horns. They went to where the pair stood. Then the wedding was promptly and cheerily performed.

Following the ceremony, merry brass bells rang. The people shouted glad hurrahs. The innocent man, followed by children dropping flowers on his path, led his bride to his home.

This was the king's semicruel method of carrying out justice. Its perfect fairness is clear. The criminal could not know out of which door would come the lady. He opened either door he wished. And he never had the slightest idea whether, in the next instant, he would be devoured or married.

Sometimes the tiger came out of one door. Sometimes it came out of the other. The decisions were not only fair, they were positively final. The accused person was instantly punished if he found himself guilty. And if innocent, he was rewarded on the spot. Whether he liked it or not. There was no escape from the judgments of the king's arena.

The trials were very popular. Many people gathered. And they never knew whether they would witness a bloody slaughter or a cheery wedding. The uncertainty made it more appealing.

So the people were entertained and pleased. And the concerned citizens couldn't bring any charge of unfairness against the plan. Because didn't the accused person have the whole matter in his own hands?

Now this semicruel king had a daughter. She was as blooming as his most elaborate ideas. And she had a soul as passionate and commanding as his own. She was the apple of her father's eye. And he loved her more than anything.

One of the king's attendants was a young man. He was a fine man but had a low rank. Just like many of the heroes of romance who loved royal maidens.

And this royal maiden loved her hero. He was more handsome and braver than any other man in the kingdom. And she was completely devoted to him.

This love affair moved along happily for many months. Until one day the king found out about it. He did not hesitate in regard to his duty. The young man was promptly thrown into prison. And a day was chosen for his trial in the king's arena.

This, of course, was an especially important occasion. His Majesty and the people were greatly interested in the trial. Never before had there been such a case. Never before had a citizen dared to love the daughter of a king.

The tiger cages of the kingdom were searched for the most savage beast. The fiercest monster would be selected for the arena.

All of the young, beautiful maidens in the kingdom were carefully examined by worthy judges. That was so the young man would have a fitting bride. Just in case fate did not determine for him a different future.

Of course, everybody knew that the deed with which the man was charged had been done. He had loved the princess. And neither he, she, nor anyone else thought of denying it.

But the king would not allow any fact of this kind to interfere with the workings of his court of judgment. Especially when he took such delight in it. No matter how it turned out, the young man would be out of his daughter's life. And the king would enjoy watching the turn of events. Those events would determine whether the young man had done wrong in loving the princess.

The appointed day arrived. The people gathered from far and near. They crowded the bleachers of the arena. Those unable to get in massed themselves against its outside walls. The king and his court were in their places, opposite the fateful twin doors.

All was ready. The signal was given. A door beneath the king opened. The lover of the princess walked into the arena. He was tall and beautiful.

A low hum sounded throughout the crowd. Most of the audience had not known that so grand a young man lived among them. No wonder the princess loved him! What a terrible thing for him to be there!

The young man went farther into the arena. Then he turned to bow to the king. It was the custom. But the young man was not thinking at all of the king. His eyes were fixed upon the princess. She sat to the right of her father.

Defying Fate

From the moment she heard about her lover's trial, the princess had thought of nothing else, night or day. She had more power, influence, and forcefulness than anyone who had ever before been interested in such a case. So she did what no other person had done—she found out the secret of the doors. She knew behind which door waited the tiger. And she knew behind which door stood the lady.

The doors were thick with heavy curtains on the inside. So it was impossible that any noise would come from within. Nothing would give a person an idea of what was inside. But gold and the power of a woman's will brought the secret to the princess.

She not only knew behind which door stood the lady. She also knew who the lady was. She was one of the loveliest damsels of the king's court. She had been selected as the reward of the accused if he was proven innocent of his crime. The princess hated her.

The princess had often seen, or imagined she saw, this lovely damsel glancing at her lover. Flirting, she thought. And sometimes the princess thought that her lover had not only noticed, but returned the glances.

Now and then she had seen them talking together. It was only for a moment or two. But a lot can be said in a short time. It could have been about the most unimportant topics. But how could she know that?

The princess hated the woman who blushed and trembled behind the silent door.

The young man turned and looked at the princess. His eyes met hers. She was paler than anyone in the vast ocean of faces around her. But he could tell by her face that she knew. She knew behind which door crouched the tiger. And behind which stood the lady.

He had expected her to know it. He understood her nature. He knew that she would never rest until she discovered the secret. The young man's only real chance for success was based on the princess's knowledge.

His quick and anxious glance asked, "Which one?" It was as plain to her as if he shouted it from where he stood. There was not an instant to be lost. The question was asked in a flash. It must be answered in another.

Her right arm lay on the cushioned armrest. She raised her hand. She made a slight, quick movement to the right. No one but her lover saw her.

He turned. Then he quickly walked across the empty space. Every heart stopped beating. Every breath was held. Every eye was fixed on the man. Without hesitating, he went to the door on the right and opened it.

Now to the point of the story. Did the tiger come out of that door? Or did the lady?

The more we think about this question, the harder it is to answer. It involves a study of the human heart. Which leads us through mazes of passion. It is often difficult to find our way out of such mazes.

Don't think of what you would do. Think of what the hotblooded princess would have done.

Despair and jealousy combined to torment her soul. She had lost her lover, but who should then have him?

So often had she thought in horror of her lover opening the door behind which waited the cruel fangs of the tiger. But how much more often had she seen him at the other door! In her daydreams she had ground her teeth and torn her hair when she saw his face in ecstasy as he opened the door of the lady!

Her soul had burned in agony when she had seen him rush to meet that woman. When she had heard the glad shouts from the crowd and the wild ringing of the happy bells. When she had seen the priest advance to the couple. And make them man and wife before her very eyes!

Wouldn't it be better for him to die at once? Then he could wait for the princess in paradise.

And yet, that awful tiger! Those shrieks! The blood!

Her decision had been shown in an instant. But it had been made after days and nights of terrible consideration. She had known she would be asked. She had decided what she would answer. And without any hesitation, she had moved her hand to the right.

The question of her decision is not to be taken lightly. And it is not for me to pretend to be the one with the answer. So I leave it up to all of you. Which came out of the opened door—the lady, or the tiger?

The

LOTTERY TICKET

*Based on
the story by
Anton Chekhov*

*A man and his wife are content with their lives
until they are faced with the possibility of wealth.
But in the end, fate hands them the lottery ticket
that they deserve. And they will never look at life
the same again.*

Ivan Dmitritch was a middle-class man. He
lived with his family on an income of 1,200
rubles a year. And he was very well satisfied with
his life.

One evening he was sitting on the sofa after
supper. He began reading the newspaper. Then
his wife Masha interrupted him.

"I forgot to look in the newspaper today," she said. "See if the list of lottery drawings is there."

Ivan looked in the paper and found the list. "Here it is," he said. "But hasn't your ticket expired?"

"No," his wife answered, "I just bought it on Tuesday."

"What is the number?" Ivan asked.

"It is in series 9,499," Masha answered. "Number 26."

"All right, I'll look," said Ivan. He scanned the list of drawings. "You said 9,499 and 26?"

"Yes," said his wife nervously.

Ivan Dmitritch had no faith in the luck of the lottery. And he wouldn't normally agree to look at the list of winning numbers. But presently he had nothing else to do. And the newspaper was right in front of his eyes. So he passed his finger downward along the column of numbers.

And it was as though luck was mocking his disbelief. Because almost immediately, at the second line from the top, his eye was caught by the figure 9,499!

Ivan couldn't believe his eyes! He quickly dropped the paper to his knees. He felt an agreeable chill in the pit of his stomach—tingling and terrible and sweet!

"Masha, 9,499 is there!" he said in a hollow voice.

His wife looked at his face. It was astonished and filled with panic. She realized he was not joking.

"Are you sure—9,499?" Masha asked. Her face turned pale. She dropped the tablecloth she'd been folding.

"Yes, yes—it really is there!" Ivan cried.

"What's the number of the ticket?" Masha asked.

"Oh, yes, there's the number of the ticket too," said Ivan. "But . . . wait! Anyway, the series of our ticket is there! You understand . . ."

Ivan looked at his wife. And he gave her a broad, senseless smile. Like when a baby is shown a bright object.

Ivan's wife smiled too. Both of them were pleased that he had only mentioned the series. That he hadn't tried to find out the number of the winning ticket. How sweet and thrilling to think of the possibility of winning!

After a long silence, Ivan spoke again. "It is our series," he said. "So there is a reasonable chance we have won. It's only a chance, but it is there!"

"Well, go ahead and look!" said Masha.

"Wait a little," advised Ivan. "We have plenty of time to be disappointed. It's on the second line from the top, so the prize is 75,000 rubles. That's not just money—it's power! In a minute I will look at the list, and—what if we really have won?"

The husband and wife began laughing. They stared at each other in silence. The possibility of winning stunned them. They couldn't think about what they could use the 75,000 for. They couldn't dream of the happiness it would bring. They could only think of the figures 9,499 and 75,000 and picture them in their imaginations.

Ivan held the paper in his hands and paced the floor. It wasn't until he had recovered from his first impression of the figures that he could begin dreaming a little.

"If we have won," he said, "it will be a new life! Of course, the ticket is yours. But if it were mine, I would, first of all, spend 25,000 on an estate. I would spend 10,000 on new furnishings, traveling, paying debts, and so on. I would put the other 40,000 in the bank to gain interest."

"Yes, an estate would be nice," his wife said as she sat down. She dropped her hands in her lap.

Pictures crowded in Ivan's imagination. Each one was even better than the last!

Ivan saw himself as well-fed, relaxed, and healthy . . .

He would be someplace warm—no, hot! He would lie on his back on the burning sand close to a stream. Or maybe he would be in the garden under a lime tree. His little boy and girl would be crawling around, digging in the sand or catching ladybugs in the grass.

Ivan would doze sweetly. He would think of nothing. Never would he need to go to the office—not today, tomorrow, or the day after. When the sun set he would take a long, hot bath. Then he would have tea with cream and rolls. In the evening he would take a walk or visit his neighbors.

"Yes, it would be nice to buy an estate," his wife said, interrupting his thoughts. It was evident by her face that she was also dreaming.

Ivan then pictured autumn. During that season he would have to take longer walks around the garden and beside the river. He would need to get thoroughly chilled so he could have a hot drink and warm up. The children would come running from the garden. They would bring a carrot and a radish that smelled of fresh earth.

Then Ivan would lie stretched full length on the sofa. He would carelessly turn the pages of a magazine. Or he would cover his face with it and give in to slumber.

But then Ivan remembered what followed summers there—cloudy, gloomy weather. It rained day and night. The bare trees wept. The wind was damp and cold.

The dogs, horses, and birds would all be wet and depressed. There would be nowhere to walk. One would have to instead pace up and down the room, looking out the gray window.

A Fate Deserved?

Ivan Dmitritch stopped and looked at his wife. "You know, I should travel, Masha," he said.

And Ivan began thinking about how nice it would be in late autumn to travel to the South of France . . . to Italy . . . to India!

"I would certainly like to travel too," said his wife. "But look at the number of the ticket!"

"Wait! Wait . . ." said Ivan.

He walked around the room and continued thinking. What if his wife really did travel? he thought. Then he could travel someplace else alone. It is pleasant to travel alone. Or in the company of light, careless women. Those who don't think and talk all the journey about their children and fret over everything.

Ivan imagined his wife in the train. She would have a number of packages and bags. She would be sighing over something. Complaining that the train made her head ache and that she had spent so much money. At the stations he would always have to be running for boiling water, bread, and butter. She wouldn't eat dinner on the train because it would be too expensive.

She would complain about every piece of money I spent, he thought. He glanced at his wife. Besides, what would be the use of her traveling? She would shut herself up in the hotel.

And she wouldn't let me out of her sight, I know!

Then, for the first time in his life, Ivan thought that his wife had grown elderly and plain. She always smelled like her cooking. While, on the other hand, he was still young, fresh, and healthy. He could easily marry again.

Yet, I will be dependent on her, he thought. I can see it now. She will lock the money up as soon as she gets it. She will look after her relations and not let me see any of the money.

Ivan thought of her relations. All those wretched brothers, sisters, aunts, and uncles would come crawling around as soon as they heard of the winning ticket. They would begin whining like beggars. They would give Ivan those oily, fake smiles.

Wretched, horrible people! If they were given anything, they would only ask for more. But if they were refused money, they would swear at Ivan and Masha. They would tell lies about them and wish them every kind of misfortune.

Then Ivan remembered his own relations. Their faces, too, now looked ugly and hateful. They are such reptiles! he thought.

And his wife's face, too, struck him as ugly and hateful. Anger swelled up in his heart against her.

She knows nothing about money, and she is so stingy, he thought. If she won it, she would give me a hundred and put the rest away under lock and key.

And he looked at his wife. Not with a smile now, but with hatred. She glanced at him too. Also with hatred and anger. She had her own daydreams, her own plans. She understood perfectly well what her husband's dreams were. She knew who would be the first to try to grab her winnings.

Her eyes seemed to scream, "It's very nice making daydreams at other people's expense! No, don't you dare!"

Her husband understood her look. Hatred began stirring in his chest. In order to annoy his wife, he glanced quickly at the fourth page of the newspaper.

To spite her, he read out in triumph, "Series 9,499, number 46! Not 26!"

Hatred and hope both disappeared instantly. At once Ivan Dmitritch and his wife thought that their house was small and dark. That the supper they had been eating was not doing them good. But instead it was lying heavy on their stomachs. That the evenings were long and wearisome . . .

"What the devil's the meaning of it?" asked Ivan, beginning to be in a bad mood. "Wherever one steps there are bits of paper under one's feet.

Crumbs, husks. The rooms are never swept! One is simply forced to go out. I condemn my soul! I should just go hang myself on the first aspen tree!"

The Myth of
PYRAMUS
and Thisbe

Fate brings two lovers together. And it forces them to desperate actions. This myth is thought to have been the basis for one of the most famous love stories of all time. Can you guess which one?

Pyramus was the handsomest young man in Babylonia. And Thisbe was the fairest maiden. Their parents lived in adjoining houses. And Pyramus and Thisbe fell in love.

Pyramus and Thisbe wanted to get married. But their parents wouldn't allow it. For their families didn't get along.

But the parents couldn't stop Pyramus and Thisbe from loving each other. They communicated through signs and glances. And the fire in their hearts burned more intensely from being covered up.

It so happened that there was a crack in the wall that separated the two properties. No one had noticed it before. But the lovers discovered it. What love won't discover! Through this crack the lovers could talk. They sent tender messages to each other.

"Cruel wall," they said. Pyramus was on one side and Thisbe on the other. "Why do you keep two lovers apart? But we are not ungrateful. We know that because of you, we can speak our loving words to each other."

They uttered such words on different sides of the wall. And when night came and they had to say good-bye, they pressed their lips upon the wall. They could come no nearer to each other.

One morning they met at their usual spot.

"Oh, dear Thisbe," said Pyramus through the crack in the wall. "Why do we have such a cruel fate that allows us to hear but not see each other?"

"I don't know," answered Thisbe. "If only we could find a way to meet."

"Well, why don't we?" asked Pyramus.

"But how?" asked Thisbe. "Our parents have forbidden us to see each other."

"They won't have to know," said Pyramus. "Tonight when everyone's asleep, we'll slip away."

"Where will we go?" asked Thisbe.

"We'll leave our houses and walk into the fields," said Pyramus.

"Where will we meet?" asked Thisbe.

"We will meet at the Tomb of Ninus, right outside the city limits," said Pyramus. "Whoever gets there first will wait for the other at the foot of a certain tree."

"I think I know the one," said Thisbe. "The white mulberry tree? The one by the fountain?"

"That's the one," answered Pyramus.

So Pyramus and Thisbe waited impatiently throughout the day for the sun to go down. And for the moon to rise. Finally, night arrived. The families retired to bed.

Thisbe carefully sneaked out of her house.

She wore a veil over her head. And she rushed to the monument in the fields.

Sitting under the tree, Thisbe looked around. Suddenly, in the dim light of the moon, she saw a lion. Its jaws dripped blood. And it was approaching the fountain to quench its thirst.

Thisbe fled. She found a safe place to hide behind a large rock. But as she was running to the rock, she dropped her veil. After the lion drank from the fountain, it turned to retreat to the woods. That's when it saw the veil. And the lion tossed and ripped it with its bloody mouth.

Pyramus had been running late. His family hadn't gone to bed as early as he had hoped. Presently he approached the meeting place.

His color washed from his cheeks. For he saw in the sand the footsteps of the lion. Then he spied the ripped, bloody veil. He naturally thought Thisbe had been killed by the lion.

"Oh, beautiful girl," cried Pyramus, "I have been the cause of your death! You, who are more worthy of life than I, have fallen the first victim. I will follow. I tempted you to a place of such great danger. And I wasn't here first to guard you. Come forth, lion, from the rocks, and tear this guilty body with your teeth!"

Then Pyramus took the veil and carried it with him to the mulberry tree. There he covered the veil with kisses and with tears.

"My blood shall also stain you," he said to the veil. And he drew out his sword and plunged it into his heart. Pyramus's blood stained all the white mulberries of the tree red.

All this time Thisbe had still been hiding behind the rock. But at this time she emerged. She was certain the lion had gone. And she didn't want to disappoint her lover.

Thisbe looked around eagerly for Pyramus. She wanted to tell him of the danger she had escaped. She approached the tree. Then she stopped.

"Surely this is not the same place," she said to herself. "For the mulberries were white, and these are red. Did I lose my way after hiding?"

While she was thinking, she looked around. And that's when she saw the body of Pyramus. He was still struggling with death.

A shudder ran through Thisbe as the ripple on still water when a sudden breeze sweeps over it. Then she screamed and ran to her lover. She embraced his body. She poured tears into his wounds and pressed kisses on his cold lips.

"Oh, Pyramus," she cried. "What has done this? Answer me, Pyramus. It is your own Thisbe who speaks. Hear me, dearest, and lift that drooping head!"

At the name of Thisbe, Pyramus opened his eyes. Then he closed them again.

Thisbe saw her veil stained with blood. Then she saw the scabbard empty of its sword.

"Your own hand has killed you and because of me," she said. "I, too, can be brave. And my love is as strong as yours. I will follow you in death. For I have been the cause. And death, which alone could part us, will not prevent my joining you. And you, unhappy parents of us both, cannot deny us our united request. As love and death have joined us, let one tomb contain us. And you, tree, don't lose the marks of slaughter. Let your berries still serve as memorials of our blood."

Saying this, she plunged the sword into her chest.

When their parents found them, they figured out what had happened. And they realized that their stubbornness had been at fault. So they granted Thisbe's wish and buried the two lovers together.

The gods also granted her wish. Forever after, the mulberry tree brought forth red berries. As it still does to this day.

The Necklace

Based on the story by Guy de Maupassant

A young woman feels that fate has failed her. After a night of pride and vanity, fate shows her another side of life. And fate has its revenge.

She was one of those girls. Pretty and charming, as though fate had made a mistake and stuck her in a family of laborers. She had no family money. No way of becoming known, understood, loved, and wedded by a man of wealth and importance.

So she let herself be married to a humble recordkeeper in the Ministry of Education. Her tastes were simple because she had never been able to afford any other.

But she was unhappy, as though she had married beneath her. She felt that she had been born for every luxury in the world. And she suffered endlessly because of it.

She suffered because of the poorness of her house. From its bare walls to its worn chairs and ugly curtains. She imagined a sitting room with Oriental rugs and lit by torches in tall bronze sockets. She imagined a vast parlor with elaborate pieces of furniture holding priceless ornaments. She imagined small, perfumed rooms created just for little parties of close friends. She dreamed of men who were famous and would make every other woman jealous.

She sat down for dinner at the round table covered with an old tablecloth. Her husband sat across from her. He took the cover off the pot of soup and said happily, "Ah! Scotch broth! What could be better?"

But she imagined delicate meals served in marvelous dishes. She imagined murmured conversation. People lingering over the rosy flesh of trout or wings of asparagus chicken.

She had no fancy clothes, no jewels, nothing. And these were the only things she loved. She felt that she was made for them.

She had a rich old school friend whom she refused to visit. Because when she returned

home, she suffered so. She would weep for days
with grief, regret, despair, and misery.

An Invitation from Fate

One evening her husband came home, looking
excited. He was holding a large envelope.

"This is for you," he said.

She quickly tore the paper and pulled out a
card. On it was printed

*The Minister of Education and Madame Ramponneau
request the pleasure of the company of Monsieur and
Madame Loisel at the Ministry on the evening of
Monday, January the 18th.*

Her husband had hoped she would be delighted.
But instead she flung the invitation across the table.

"What do you want me to do with this?" she
asked.

"Why, darling," her husband answered. "I
thought you'd be pleased. You never get to go
out. This is a great occasion. I went to a lot of
trouble to get the invitation. Everyone wants one.
It's very select. Very few recordkeepers get one.
You'll see all the really big people there."

She looked at him with furious eyes. "And
what do you suppose I am to wear at such an
occasion?" she asked.

He had not thought about that. He stammered,
"Why, the dress you go to the theater in. It looks
very nice to me . . ."

He stopped. For his wife was beginning to cry. Two large tears ran slowly down her face.

"What's the matter with you?" he asked.

In a dramatic way she overcame her grief. She wiped her wet cheeks and replied, "Nothing. Except I don't have a dress. So I can't go to this party. Give your invitation to some friend of yours whose wife will look better than I will."

He was heartbroken.

"Look here, Mathilde," he said. "How much would a suitable dress cost? One which you could use on other occasions as well? Something very simple?"

She thought for several seconds. She was wondering for how large a sum she could ask without receiving an immediate refusal.

At last she replied with some hesitation, "I don't know exactly. But I think I could do it for 400 francs."

He grew slightly pale. For this was exactly the amount he had been saving for a gun. He was intending to do a little hunting next summer with some friends.

But he said, "Very well. I will give you 400 francs. But try to get a really nice dress with the money."

Days later Madame Loisel's dress was ready. However, she seemed sad and uneasy. The day of the party drew near.

One evening her husband said to her, "What's the matter with you? You've been acting very funny for the last three days."

"I am miserable," she replied. "Because I don't have any jewels, not a single stone, to wear. I would almost rather not go to the party."

"Wear flowers," her husband suggested. "They're very pretty this time of year. For ten francs you could get two or three gorgeous roses."

But she was not convinced.

"No," she said. "There's nothing worse than looking poor in the middle of a room of rich women."

"I know!" exclaimed her husband. "Go and see Madame Forestier and ask her to lend you some jewels. You know her quite well enough for that."

Madame Loisel uttered a cry of delight.

"That's true!" she cried. "I never thought of it!"

The next day she went to see her friend. She told her of her trouble.

Madame Forestier went to her dressing table. She lifted a large box and handed it to Madame Loisel.

"Choose, my dear," said Madame Forestier.

First Madame Loisel saw some bracelets. Then a pearl necklace. Then a cross in gold and gems. She tried on each one in front of the mirror. But she was unable to make up her mind.

"Don't you have anything else?" she asked.

"Yes, look for yourself," said Madame Forestier. "I don't know what you would like best."

Suddenly Madame Loisel discovered it. It was in a black satin case—a superb diamond necklace. Her heart began to pound. Her hands trembled as she lifted it. She fastened it around her neck and rejoiced at the sight of herself.

With hesitation, she asked, "Could you lend me this, just this alone?"

"Yes, of course," said Madame Forestier.

Madame Loisel flung her arms around her friend's neck. Then she went away with her treasure.

The day of the party arrived. And Madame Loisel was a success. She was the prettiest woman there. She was elegant and graceful. She smiled constantly.

All the men stared at her. They asked to be introduced to her. All the Under-Secretaries of State were eager to waltz with her. The Minister even noticed her.

She danced madly, with no thought of anything. She triumphed in her beauty and in her success.

She left about 4:00 in the morning. Since midnight her husband had been dozing in a deserted little room. Along with three other men whose wives were having a good time.

He threw over her shoulders the coat he had

brought for her to go home in. It was a modest, everyday coat. Its poverty clashed with the beauty of her ball dress.

She wanted to hurry away. She didn't want to be noticed by the other women putting on their costly furs.

Monsieur Loisel stopped her. "Wait a minute," he said. "You'll catch cold in the open. I'm going to get a cab."

But she did not listen to him. She quickly descended the staircase.

When they were out in the street, they could not find a cab right away. So they walked down toward the Seine River. They were desperate and shivering.

At last they managed to hail a cab. It took them to the door of their building. Sadly, they walked up to their own apartment.

She was thinking that it was the end for her. He was thinking that he had to be at the office at 10:00.

Fate's Cruel Joke

When they got inside their apartment, she took off the coat in which she had wrapped her shoulders. She wanted to see herself in all her glory in front of the mirror.

But all of a sudden she uttered a cry. The necklace was no longer around her neck!

"What's the matter with you?" asked her husband.

She turned toward him with a look of distress.

"I . . . I . . . I no longer have Madame Forestier's necklace . . ."

He stared at her. He couldn't believe it.

"What?!" he exclaimed. "Impossible!"

They searched in the folds of her dress. And in the folds of her coat. They looked in her pockets—everywhere. But they could not find it.

"Are you sure you still had it on when you left the ball?" he asked.

"Yes," she said. "I touched it as we were leaving."

"But if you lost it in the street, we would have heard it fall," he said.

"Yes, you're right," she said. "Did you get the number of the cab?"

"No," he said. "You didn't notice, did you?"

"No," she answered.

Then they stared at each other. Monsieur Loisel put his coat on again. "I'll go over all the ground we walked," he said. "I'll see if I can find it."

So he went out. She stayed in her ball dress. She didn't have the strength to change or get into bed. She was terrified.

Her husband returned about 7:00. He had found nothing.

He then went to the police station, the newspapers, and the cab companies to offer a reward.

Madame Loisel waited all day long. She was still in a state of shock at what was happening.

Her husband came home that night. His face was lined and pale. He had discovered nothing.

"You must write to your friend," he said. "Tell her that you've broken the clasp of her necklace and are getting it fixed. That will give us more time to look."

So she wrote the letter.

But by the end of the week, they had lost all hope.

Monsieur Loisel, who had aged five years, declared, "We must see about replacing the diamond necklace."

They looked inside the box that the necklace had been in. There they saw the name of a jeweler. So they took the box to him.

He looked through his books. "I did not sell this necklace," he said. "I must have just supplied the clasp."

The husband and wife then went from jeweler to jeweler. They searched for another necklace like the first. They both tried to remember exactly what the necklace looked like.

Finally in a small shop they found a string of diamonds. It seemed to be exactly like the one they were looking for. It was worth 40,000 francs. But the jeweler said he would sell it to them for 36,000.

They begged the jeweler not to sell it for three days. And the jeweler agreed that if the first necklace were found before the first of February, he would buy back his string of diamonds for 34,000 francs.

Monsieur Loisel had 18,000 francs that was left to him by his father. He would have to borrow the rest.

And borrow it he did. He got 1,000 from one man and 500 from another. He entered into risky agreements and did business with loan sharks and a whole tribe of moneylenders. He mortgaged everything he had. And he didn't know if he could ever pay it all back.

Then, with an agonizing thought of the future, he went back to the jeweler's. And he put on the counter 36,000 francs.

Madame Loisel took the necklace back to Madame Forestier. Madame Forestier said, "You should have brought it back sooner. I might have needed it."

Madame Loisel feared that her friend would open the case. What if she noticed the substitution? What would she say? Would she think her friend was a thief?

But Madame Forestier did not open the case.

Madame Loisel came to know the life of extreme poverty. But she played her part like a heroine. She knew that the fearful debt must be paid off. And she would pay it. She dismissed her servant. They rented a room in an attic.

She came to know the heavy work of the house. She washed the dishes and wore out her pink nails on the bottoms of pans. She washed the clothes and hung them to dry on a string. Dressed like a poor woman, she went to the grocer, butcher, and market. Then she fought to save every halfpenny.

Every month they paid their debts.

Her husband worked in the evenings straightening out a merchant's accounts. Some nights he did copying after that.

And this life lasted ten years.

At the end of the ten years, everything was paid off.

Madame Loisel looked old now. She had become like all the other strong, coarse women of poor households. Her hair was badly done. Her skirts were tattered. Her hands were red. She spoke in a shrill voice. The water now slopped all over the floor when she scrubbed it.

But sometimes when her husband was at the office, she would sit by the window and think.

She would think about that evening long ago.

She would think of the ball. She had been so beautiful and so admired.

What would have happened if she had never lost those jewels? she wondered. Who knows?

One Sunday she decided to go for a walk. She needed to freshen herself after her labors of the week. She suddenly caught sight of a woman who was taking a child out for a walk. It was Madame Forestier. She was still young and still beautiful.

Madame Loisel became nervous. Should she speak to her? Yes, certainly. And now that she had paid her debts, she would tell her everything. Why not?

She went up to Madame Forestier.

"Good morning, Jeanne," she said.

The woman did not recognize her. And she was surprised at being so familiarly addressed by a poor woman.

"But . . . Madame," Madame Forestier stammered. "I don't know you . . . you must be making a mistake."

"No . . . I am Madame Loisel," she said.

Her friend uttered a cry.

"Oh! My poor Mathilde," said Madame Forestier, "how you have changed!"

"Yes, I've had some hard times since I last saw you," said Madame Loisel. "And all because of you."

"Because of me?" her friend asked. "How was that?"

"You remember the diamond necklace you lent me for the ball at the Ministry?" Madame Loisel asked.

"Yes," said her friend. "Well?"

"Well," said Madame Loisel, "I lost it."

"But you brought it back," said Madame Forestier. She was confused.

"I bought you another one just like it," said Madame Loisel. "And for the last ten years I've been paying for it. It wasn't easy for us. We had no money. But it's paid for at last. And I'm glad."

Madame Forestier was silent for a moment.

"You say you bought a diamond necklace to replace mine?" she finally asked.

"Yes," said her friend. "You hadn't noticed? They were very much alike."

Then Madame Loisel smiled in proud and innocent happiness.

Madame Forestier became very emotional. She grabbed both of Madame Loisel's hands.

"Oh, my poor Mathilde!" she cried. "But mine was an imitation. It was worth at the very most 500 francs!"

The Play

Cast

Narrator	Guest 1
Madame Loisel	Guest 2
Monsieur Loisel	Jeweler 1
Madame Forestier	Jeweler 2

Setting: 19th-century France

Act One

Narrator: She was one of those girls. Pretty and charming, as though fate had made a mistake and stuck her in a family of laborers. She had no family money. No way of becoming known, understood, loved, and wedded by a man of wealth and importance.

So she let herself be married to a humble recordkeeper in the Ministry of Education. Her tastes were simple because she had never been able to afford any other.

But she was unhappy, as though she had married beneath her. She felt that she had been born for every luxury in the world. And she suffered endlessly because of it.

Madame Loisel: I hate the poorness of this house. Just look at its bare walls, its worn chairs, and its ugly curtains. I imagine instead a sitting room. One with Oriental rugs and lit by torches in tall bronze sockets. And a vast parlor with elaborate pieces of furniture holding priceless ornaments. And small, perfumed rooms. Ones created just for parties of close friends. Especially famous men who would make every other woman jealous.

Narrator: She sat down for dinner at the round table covered with an old tablecloth. Her husband sat across from her. He took the cover off the pot of soup.

Monsieur Loisel: Ah! Scotch broth! What could be better?

Madame Loisel: I know what could be better. Delicate meals served in marvelous dishes. Murmured conversation. People lingering over the rosy flesh of trout or wings of asparagus chicken.

Narrator: She had no fancy clothes, no jewels, nothing. And these were the only things she loved. She felt that she was made for them.

She had a rich old school friend whom she refused to visit. Because when she returned home, she suffered so. She would weep for days with grief, regret, despair, and misery.

Act Two

Narrator: One evening her husband came home looking excited. He was holding a large envelope.

Monsieur Loisel: This is for you.

Narrator: She quickly tore the paper and pulled out a card. She read what it said.

Madame Loisel: "The Minister of Education and Madame Ramponneau request the pleasure of the company of Monsieur and Madame Loisel at the Ministry on the evening of Monday, January the 18th."

Narrator: Her husband had hoped she would be delighted. But instead she flung the invitation across the table.

Madame Loisel: What do you want me to do with this?

Monsieur Loisel: Why, darling, I thought you'd be pleased. You never get to go out. This is a great occasion. I went to a lot of trouble to get the invitation. Everyone wants one. It's very select. Very few recordkeepers get one. You'll see all the really big people there.

Madame Loisel: And what do you suppose I am to wear at such an occasion?

Monsieur Loisel: I . . . I had not thought about that . . . Why, the dress you go to the theater in. It looks very nice to me . . .

Narrator: He stopped. For his wife was beginning to cry. Two large tears ran slowly down her face.

Monsieur Loisel: What's the matter with you?

Narrator: In a dramatic way she overcame her grief. She wiped her wet cheeks.

Madame Loisel: Nothing. Except I don't have a dress. So I can't go to this party. Give your invitation to some friend of yours whose wife will look better than I will.

Narrator: He was heartbroken.

Monsieur Loisel: Look here, Mathilde. How much would a suitable dress cost? One which you could use on other occasions as well? Something very simple?

Narrator: She thought for several seconds. She was wondering for how large a sum she could ask without receiving an immediate refusal.

Madame Loisel: I don't know exactly. But I think I could do it for 400 francs.

Narrator: He grew slightly pale. For this was exactly the amount he had been saving for a gun. He was intending to do a little hunting next summer with some friends.

Monsieur Loisel: Very well. I will give you 400 francs. But try to get a really nice dress with the money.

Narrator: Days later Madame Loisel's dress was ready. However, she seemed sad and uneasy. The day of the party grew near.

Monsieur Loisel: What's the matter with you? You've been acting very funny for the last three days.

Madame Loisel: I am miserable because I don't have any jewels, not a single stone, to wear. I would almost rather not go to the party.

Monsieur Loisel: Why don't you wear flowers? They're very pretty this time of year. For ten francs you could get two or three gorgeous roses.

Madame Loisel: No. There's nothing worse than looking poor in the middle of a room of rich women.

Monsieur Loisel: I know! Go and see Madame Forestier and ask her to lend you some jewels. You know her quite well enough for that.

Madame Loisel: That's true! I never thought of it!

Narrator: The next day she went to see her friend. She told her of her trouble.
Madame Forestier went to her dressing table. She lifted a large box and handed it to Madame Loisel.

Madame Forestier: Choose, my dear.

Madame Loisel: Ooh, I want to try those bracelets. No, this pearl necklace. Oh, here's a cross in gold and gems!

Narrator: Madame Loisel tried on each one in front of the mirror. But she was unable to make up her mind.

Madame Loisel: Don't you have anything else?

Madame Forestier: Yes, look for yourself. I don't know what you would like best.

Narrator: Suddenly Madame Loisel discovered it. It was in a black satin case—a superb diamond necklace. Her heart began to pound. Her hands trembled as she lifted it. She fastened it around her neck and rejoiced at the sight of herself.

Madame Loisel: Could you lend me this, just this alone?

Madame Forestier: Yes, of course.

Madame Loisel: Oh, thank you! You are a true friend!

Act Three

Narrator: The day of the party arrived. And Madame Loisel was a success.

Guest 1: Who is that woman? She's the prettiest one here. She's elegant and graceful. And her smile lights up the room.

Guest 2: I don't know. But I haven't been able to keep my eyes off her all evening. I am going to ask to be introduced to her. I will not rest until I have waltzed with her.

Narrator: The Minister himself even noticed her. She danced madly, with no thought of anything. She triumphed in her beauty and in her success.

She left about 4:00 in the morning. Since midnight her husband had been dozing in a deserted little room. Along with three other men whose wives were having a good time.

He threw over her shoulders the coat he had brought for her to go home in. It was a modest, everyday coat. Its poverty clashed with the beauty of her ball dress.

Madame Loisel: Let's hurry away. Before any of the women in their costly furs notice me.

Monsieur Loisel: Wait a minute. You'll catch cold in the open. I'm going to get a cab.

Narrator: But she did not listen to him. She quickly descended the staircase.

Monsieur Loisel: Where are all the cabs tonight?

Madame Loisel: Oh, I'm shivering. It's so cold!

Monsieur Loisel: Let's walk down toward the Seine River. Ah, finally a cab.

Narrator: The cab took them to the door of their building. Sadly, they walked up to their own apartment.

She was thinking that it was the end for her. He was thinking that he had to be at the office at 10:00.

Madame Loisel: I am going to take off this hideous wrap. I want to see myself in all my glory in front of the mirror one last time. What?! It can't be!

Monsieur Loisel: What's the matter with you?

Madame Loisel: I . . . I . . . I no longer have Madame Forestier's necklace . . .

Monsieur Loisel: What?! Impossible! It has to be on your clothing somewhere.

Narrator: They searched in the folds of her dress. And in the folds of her coat. They looked in her pockets—everywhere. But they could not find it.

Monsieur Loisel: Are you sure you still had it on when you left the ball?

Madame Loisel: Yes, I touched it as we were leaving.

Monsieur Loisel: But if you lost it in the street, we would have heard it fall.

Madame Loisel: Yes, you're right. Did you get the number of the cab?

Monsieur Loisel: No. You didn't notice, did you?

Madame Loisel: No.

Monsieur Loisel: I'll go over all the ground we walked. I'll see if I can find it.

Narrator: So he went out. She stayed in her ball dress. She didn't have the strength to change or get into bed. She was terrified.

Her husband returned about 7:00.

Madame Loisel: Well, did you find it?

Monsieur Loisel: No. I looked everywhere. I'll go to the police station, the newspapers, and the cab companies to offer a reward. Maybe it will turn up.

Narrator: She waited all day long. She was still in a state of shock at what was happening.

Her husband came home that night. His face was lined and pale. He had discovered nothing.

Monsieur Loisel: You must write to your friend. Tell her that you've broken the clasp of her necklace and are getting it fixed. That will give us more time to look.

Narrator: So she wrote the letter. But by the end of the week, they had lost all hope.

Monsieur Loisel: We must see about replacing the diamond necklace.

Madame Loisel: The name of a jeweler is inside the box the necklace was in. We should take the box to him.

Narrator: The couple found the jeweler. But he wasn't much help.

Jeweler 1: I've looked through my books. I did not sell this necklace. I must've just supplied the clasp.

Narrator: The couple then went from jeweler to jeweler. They searched for another necklace like the first. They both tried to remember exactly what the necklace looked like.

Jeweler 2: Hmm. I think I have what you are describing. Here is a string of diamonds that appears to be very similar.

Monsieur Loisel: Yes, that looks right. Don't you think so, Mathilde?

Madame Loisel: Yes, that's it! How much is it?

Jeweler 2: It's worth 40,000 francs.

Monsieur Loisel: Oh, my. Where will we ever get that kind of money?

Jeweler 2: If it will help, I will sell it to you for 36,000.

Monsieur Loisel: Thank you. I'm sure that will help some. Tell me, could you please hold it for us for three days? That will give us time to come up with the money.

Jeweler 2: I suppose I could do that for you. But if you do not come back after three days, I will have to sell it to someone else.

Madame Loisel: What if we find the original necklace? Will you take this one back?

Jeweler 2: I do not give refunds. But, because of your situation, if you find it before the first of February, I will give you 34,000 francs back.

Monsieur Loisel: Thank you, sir. We will be back.

Jeweler 2: Good-bye.

Madame Loisel: Oh, how will we ever come up with the money?

Monsieur Loisel: I have 18,000 francs in savings that my father left me. I will have to borrow the rest.

Narrator: And borrow it he did. He got 1,000 from one man and 500 from another. He entered into risky agreements and did business with loan sharks and a whole tribe of moneylenders. He mortgaged everything he had. And he didn't know if he could ever pay it all back.

Then, with an agonizing thought of the future, he went back to the jeweler's. And he put on the counter 36,000 francs.

Madame Loisel: Madame Forestier, here is your necklace back. I fixed the clasp for you.

Madame Forestier: You should have brought it back sooner. I might have needed it.

Narrator: Madame Loisel feared that her friend would open the case. What if she noticed the substitution? What would she say? Would she think her friend was a thief?

But Madame Forestier did not open the case.

Act Four

Narrator: Madame Loisel came to know the life of extreme poverty. But she played her part like a heroine.

Madame Loisel: The fearful debt must be paid off. And I will pay it. I will dismiss my servant. And we will rent a room in an attic.

Narrator: She came to know the heavy work of the house. She washed the dishes and wore out her pink nails on the bottoms of pans. She washed the clothes and hung them to dry on a string. Dressed like a poor woman, she went to the grocer, butcher, and market. Then she fought to save every halfpenny.

Every month they paid their debts.

Monsieur Loisel: Mathilde, I will work extra jobs to help pay the debt. I have agreed to work in the evenings to straighten out a merchant's accounts. And I can do some copying after that.

Narrator: And this life lasted ten years. At the end of ten years, everything was paid off.

Madame Loisel: How old I look now! I have become like all the other strong, coarse women of poor households. My hair is badly done. My skirts are tattered. My hands are red. I speak in a shrill voice. The water now slops all over the floor when I scrub it.

Ah, but to think about that evening long ago! The ball! I was so beautiful and so admired. What would have happened if I had never lost those jewels? Who knows?

Narrator: One Sunday she decided to go for a walk.

Madame Loisel: I need to freshen myself after my labors of the week. Why, who is that woman taking that child out on a walk? She looks familiar. I don't believe it! It's Madame Forestier. She is still young and still beautiful. Should I speak to her? Yes, certainly. And now that I have paid my debts, I will tell her everything. Why not?

Good morning, Jeanne.

Narrator: The woman did not recognize her. And she was surprised at being so familiarly addressed by a poor woman.

Madame Forestier: But . . . Madame, I don't know you . . . you must be making a mistake.

Madame Loisel: No . . . I am Madame Loisel.

Madame Forestier: Oh, my poor Mathilde! How you have changed!

Madame Loisel: Yes, I've had some hard times since I last saw you. And all because of you.

Madame Forestier: Because of me? How was that?

Madame Loisel: You remember the diamond necklace you lent me for the ball at the Ministry?

Madame Forestier: Yes. Well?

Madame Loisel: Well, I lost it.

Madame Forestier: But you brought it back. I don't understand.

Madame Loisel: I bought you another one just like it. And for the last ten years I've been paying for it. It wasn't easy for us. We had no money. But it's paid for at last. And I'm glad.

Narrator: Madame Forestier was silent for a moment.

Madame Forestier: You say you bought a diamond necklace to replace mine?

Madame Loisel: Yes, you hadn't noticed? They were very much alike.

Narrator: Then Madame Loisel smiled in proud and innocent happiness.
Madame Forestier became very emotional. She grabbed both of Madame Loisel's hands.

Madame Forestier: Oh, my poor Mathilde! But mine was an imitation. It was worth, at the very most, 500 francs!